A LIFE OF CRIME

ARON BEAUREGARD

ISBN: 978-1-961758-99-5

Cover & Interior Art by Anton Rosovsky

Cover wrap design by Aron Beauregard

Edited by Jason Parent

Printed in the USA

WARNING:
This book contains scenes and subject matter that are disgusting and disturbing; easily offended people are not the intended audience.

JOIN MY MAILING LIST NOW
FOR EXCLUSIVE OFFERS BY VISITING:
substack.com/@abhorror

FOR SIGNED BOOKS, MERCHANDISE,
AND EXCLUSIVE ITEMS VISIT:

www.ABHorror.com

This book is for the people who came to the fork in the road and finally went straight.

I'm glad you made it.

*And for my wife, who hung out with me while I wrote it.
I love you.*

AB HORROR

POCKET ATROCITIES

FOR SIGNED BOOKS, MERCH, AND
EXCLUSIVE ITEMS FROM ARON BEAUREGARD, VISIT

ABHORROR.COM

FERTILIZED EGGS

Shane McKenzie, June 2024

Do you believe in fate? How about destiny?

I do... kind of.

You're probably thinking, "Aren't those the same fucking thing, asshole?"

Well, allow me to share with you the results of my "destiny vs fate" Google search that I just did: Fate is typically used to refer to events or outcomes that are predetermined and beyond one's control, while destiny is used to refer to a predetermined outcome or path that a person or thing is destined to follow.

That clear it up for you?!

Yeah, me neither. Let me try and put this into my own dumbass, mostly uneducated words.

I believe that certain things are destined to happen or meant to be, but that one's choices in life can steer things away from that destiny. And what's fucked up is, sometimes it seems like it's the bad choices that you make that end up, in the long run, actually being the exact choice you had to make to stay on that destined path.

For example, I am a very happily married man who loves his wife so very much. I went to college and earned an associate's degree (hold your applause, I'm just a man) in computer animation. Not exciting enough for you? I specialized in 3-D environment modeling... ooohhhhh! Anyways, immediately after my graduation, I was offered a job at a video game company in Dallas, TX. I thought to myself, *Well goddamn, that was easy. If I got a job offer before I could even take off my cap and gown, then I'll just go back home to Austin, and I'll have to turn down offers!*

Yeah... I didn't just hear crickets, those little fuckers were playing violins too. So I did what any twenty-two-year-old artist with a fresh college degree would do. I moved in with my parents and asked my dad to help me get a job where he worked: the Austin Police Department. I nepo-babied the shit outta that, got a job as a 9-1-1 call taker, and spent every day hating myself for not taking that job in Dallas.

Well guess who I met at that job? Twenty years, and two kids, later, I'm living an amazing life with the person I love most, and I would argue it took a boneheaded decision on my part to get here.

Even if our choices aren't so easily trackable, could it be that if we'd changed even the smallest thing, our fates/destinies would have turned out completely different? You know, the buttermilk effect or whatever.

Let me hit you with one more example (because if I keep going, Aron will get mad at me for writing a long-ass intro after I told him it would probably be two pages or so). I'll keep this one short and to the point.

I started writing fiction in 2010 and my first book was published in 2012. I had a lot of success very fast (to the chagrin of many) which led me to screenwriting. I started writing short films in 2013, had my book *Muerte*

Con Carne adapted into a film in 2014, which led to me being hired to write a web series for Warner Bros. in 2017. At this point, I was focusing more on my screenwriting than writing books because of... well, because of money. I could write a script in about as much time as it took me to write a book, and I would make about 8,000% more money (I had to Google that too. Just cuz I'm Asian don't mean I'm good at math. Stop being racist, Aron).

At one point, I had to make the decision to leave books behind so I could spend all my energy on building my screenwriting career, which was going really well. I wrote a movie for Sony... which got killed by Covid, but I still wrote it dammit!

I conceptualized and wrote a movie for Blumhouse and Amazon Studios called *Bingo Hell* which somehow led to me getting hired to rewrite a biopic written by the woman who wrote *What's Love Got to Do With It?* Makes total sense, right?

Things were going well. I had a team of agents, a manager, an entertainment attorney, and my Writer's Guild of America card. And then... the motherfucking strike happened.

The momentum was halted for multiple projects in the works, many of which ultimately died as a result. I was forbidden to do any screenwriting work, including work I was already contracted to do.

After a few months of this, Killercon happened. Killercon, if you don't know, is an extreme horror writer's convention put on by one of my best friends in this world, Wrath James White. And on this particular year, a dude named Aron Beauregard was a guest of honor. Let me cut to the chase here.

I hadn't written a book in about eight years. Aron and Kristopher Triana approached me and invited me to write with them (I'm not sure I'm allowed to say yet, but if you know you know). I agreed because, for one, I needed to write and wasn't allowed to write movies. But more importantly, I fucking missed writing books. I missed the creative freedom... I missed being in control of my own ideas! And as much as I love writing movies, there are more cooks in the kitchen than a season of Master Chef.

I took a trip to Rhode Island and stayed with Aron for a few days, and he caught me up on the business and everything I'd missed while I was busy getting fingerbanged by Hollywood. And he made me remember why I started writing in the first place: because I fucking love telling stories! Not for money or IMDB credits or fancy fucking movie premieres. It all came full circle, right back to where I started.

Where I rediscovered my spark and passion. Where I write what I want the way I want. Where I'm fucking happy.

If that shit ain't destiny or fate, then I don't know what is. Sometimes that shit is messy and confusing and devastating and traumatizing, but maybe there is some kind of divine design to all this.

Maybe, like the protagonist of this book, you can deny your fate, make choice after choice to give yourself the illusion of being in control, but it just might all come full circle, and whether you like it or not, you're destined to fulfill your fate.

After all, aren't we all just fertilized eggs in constant danger of being scrambled, poached, or boiled hard by this hungry, predatory world? Sooner or later, we either rot away or get eaten. The choice is yours.

Or is it?

NOW ONLY
15¢
A LIFE OF CRIME
ARON BEAUREGARD

SHOPLIFTING

Harvey Sutton, November 1981

I'd have sucked the cashier's cock for that can of Spam. I tried not to act too suspicious. The guy'd been watching me since I walked in and for good reason. I just had that look about me.

I looked like a scumbag.

With some people, you can just tell with the eyeball test. There's a certain aura about us. It ain't that I was trying to seem like a scumbag. The world—and people who never looked out for me in it— made me this way. After all, I was just fifteen years old. What else was I supposed to do?

Sucking cock wasn't the worst thing, especially if you were willing. For me, it wasn't that big of a deal. I'd been doing it since before I ran away from the boy's home anyhow. I wasn't doing it cuz I liked it—I ain't a faggot or nothin'—I just did it to survive.

There were a few adults inside that fuckin' boy's home who were sick. Doing things that no kid should experience. But I didn't know no better. Even after I'd left, I didn't realize how wrong it was. How much it twisted up a young mind.

I'm surprised so many of the other kids in that place decided to stick around. Not me though, I'd rather be cold and alone than under someone else's thumb. I was tired of bein' treated like a goddamn toy.

But, in comparison to my parents, that temporary home was a walk in the park. I'd rather suck cock than get beat any day of the week. My mom and dad weren't good for each other. They sure as shit never planned on havin' me— made it obvious when I lived with 'em. When they weren't beatin' the piss out of me, they were telling me what a mistake I was. There was no sexual shit with them, but unlike the sexual shit at the boy's home that was only once in a while, the beatings and mental abuse were pretty much every day.

When they weren't goin' in on me, they were goin' in on each other. Until one morning, I woke up before my folks did. They were early birds so that was kinda weird. Eventually, I heard someone laughing. I followed the trail of giggles to my parents' bedroom and found my mom sitting on the bed staring out the window.

Her body was rumbling from her amusement. It took me a second to notice, but my dad was still in bed. When I seen the blood all over the comforter and the puddle on the top of his chest, I felt nothing. Not fear, not disgust, not relief, not sadness.

Nothing.

I still wondered about Mom from time to time—what prison was like for her or if she was even still alive. But I was usually more concerned with figuring out how the fuck I was gonna keep warm or fill my belly.

But havin' to steal and scrap to survive became a welcomed act. At least I didn't have to worry about going home to my parents or the boy's home.

The streets were my home.

My gaze darted to the cashier. He was a long-haired hippie-type. The guy was really eyeballin' the shit out of me. I moved past the Spam so I didn't seem too focused on it. I was hoping that Donya would hurry the fuck up, but she'd never been reliable.

The song playing on the radio changed right when I turned around. As I looked at the newsstand, I saw and heard Bianca Blush. At that moment, she was the hottest thing in music, gracing many of the magazine covers on the display in front of me. Her hit single, 'Make You Blush' bled out of the radio.

I didn't get a chance to listen to much music, mostly whatever other people had on. The pop stuff wasn't my thing, but I always rooted for Bianca Blush. She was probably the only person from our shitty city to do anything noteworthy.

I'd heard stories about her before she'd found any kind of success in the music industry. She started in the streets, just like me. In a way, seeing her on all of them covers gave me hope. If she'd scraped and clawed her way out of the drug dens, violence, and cold alleyways, maybe I could do the same. Also, it didn't hurt that she was fuckin' hot too.

"Ugh, I hate this fuckin' song," the cashier grumbled.

When the door swung open, I was glad to see, at least at that moment, I could count on Donya. She looked the way she always did—her short braids were a bit crusty, face curled by a perpetual frown, and eyes bugged out. Donya's head was naturally misshapen, and her teeth looked a little sharper than most people's did.

I don't know exactly what was wrong with her, but I think whatever issues she had happened in the womb. She never did tell me a whole lot about herself, she was kind of secretive. I got that. I wasn't someone who liked talkin' about all the fucked-up shit that happened to me much either. It was easier to just try and forget about it or pretend it hadn't happened.

The one nugget she did share with me about her past was that her mom was a heavy drug user. Donya believed that her doin' all that shit while she was pregnant was what fucked her up. And, to me, that seemed about right. That's about all I knew. She hadn't told me how she'd become homeless or anything else.

Donya Mims was a mystery.

Still, workin' with her when she did show up always paid off. Donya was a great distraction. Being a white boy, whenever someone with darker skin walked into the store, the cashier's attention immediately shifted to them. Even though I had that scumbag look, those judgmental pricks couldn't help themselves. We made a good team—she lured 'em in while I robbed 'em blind.

"Yo, mister," Donya said, looking at the cashier with her bug eyes and cupping her hand over her backside. "Where the bafroom at? I gotta take a shit."

"The restroom is for *paying* customers only," the cashier said, a look of disgust twisting his lip.

I bent slightly toward the shelf behind me, still looking at the magazine rack. Carefully, I extended my fingers and slipped the can of Spam into my back pocket.

"Man, fuck you," Donya said, sucking her teeth. "Who is you to tell me where to shit? I'll drop my drawers right here if I want."

She walked over to the far side of the store, putting her fingers over her jogging pants, threatening to do it.

"Hey!" the cashier yelled. "Damn it!" He rushed forward, maneuvering around the counter toward her. "Don't you dare!"

"Or what?" Donya asked.

I quietly slipped out the door while the guy was distracted by Donya's antics.

When I got into the alley, I waited for Donya before opening the can. Back then, I wasn't fully committed to a life of crime. I was just doing what I needed to get by.

It was Thanksgiving morning, and I wasn't about to go hungry on the same day all the other bloated fucks in our upside-down country were busy stuffing their faces.

When Donya made it to the alley, I surprised her with something I'd stashed a day earlier. She almost cried when I showed her the can of baked beans.

I popped open the Spam's top and the cube of meat slid out, accompanied by an orange, gelatinous slime.

Food was food to me. Whether it was cold or hot or tasted like shit didn't matter. I'd learned at a young age that it was really all about nourishment. Having enough energy to battle the cold and draw up our next scheme. It was about survival.

After breaking it down the middle, I handed half of the meat block to Donya and kept the other half for myself. For people like us, that Thanksgiving was one of the better ones. We hadn't gotten pinched for stealin', and I was grateful to have something to eat.

BREAKING AND ENTERING

Harvey Sutton, July 1983

Me and Donya went to the warehouse sometimes to get away. The streets were so chaotic. If it wasn't one thing, it was another. People gettin' shot, stabbed, raped, and mugged was the norm. Every once in a while, we both got tired of constantly looking over our shoulders. We just wanted a place to feel safe.

Some old mill buildings sat on the outskirts of the city, too far out for lazy junkies and ruthless gangsters to make their way out to. There was a certain amount of privacy there, but such a troop couldn't be taken without preparation.

I'd gathered up some food the prior week—mostly canned stuff I'd lifted off the back of grocery trucks because it traveled well. Donya did her part lifting a sheet of acid off this drug dealer who got a little too loaded at a party. She was always wild like that. It was a ballsy move, but she was a ballsy broad. The type you wouldn't wanna have to meet in a dark alley or scrap with.

Trippin' was the closest thing street people like us could get to a vacation. With the stress and grueling survival routine we dealt with on the regular, I was excited when we were finally set up inside.

A part of me was kind of depressed about our whole situation, though. I'd tried—we both did—to look for the light at the end of the tunnel. But it just seemed like there was no way to get off the streets.

Once the streets had a hold of you, locating a shelter from the violence and seductive vices was pretty much impossible. When you're caught up in the drug game, someone's always lookin' to put the hurt on you. It felt like we were both lookin' for a path to being a regular person, but that path just didn't exist for us.

All I wanted was to be someone who had a place to live, maybe a small group of people who noticed when I wasn't around, and a job to stabilize us. But reality was harsh.

No one wants to hire a skill-less man who smells like shit and a bitch who acts as crazy as she looks. All we could offer was toughness, nothing that was actually useful in the working industries. So we just stayed in the gutter, doing the grimy shit people in the gutter do. Which is why we were in that warehouse.

We started a fire in a trash can that we'd used on several prior occasions. Bullshitting a bit, we drank on some 40s of malt liquor, waiting for nightfall. We both liked to wait for the darkness before we dropped the LSD. That kind of environment usually made our 'vacation' more intense.

Donya polished off her beer and threw the bottle in the fire. "How much you finna take?"

"Half," I replied.

"Half a tab? That ain't gonna do shit."

"No, half the sheet."

Her eyes went extra wide. "Damn. I don't know bout that."

"Well I do."

"I'm not so sure you should."

"Why? The fuck I got to worry about?"

"J-Roc was braggin' bout this shit." She reached into her pocket for the sheet.

I shrugged. "So what, J-Roc brags about everythin'. He's a storyteller."

"Nah, I mean he was makin' it sound like it wasn't *just* some LSD. He made it sound like it was some new type shit. Like some people was comin' back from their trips different."

"That's what I'm bettin' on," I said.

"Whatchu mean?"

I threw my empty bottle into the barrel, cracked a fresh 40 oz, and guzzled. "I mean I ain't for this world. I'm more in touch with all that alien shit I see in there than this place, any day of the week."

"I know, but half a sheet is gonna be some bugged-out shit."

"I been doing all kinda shit since I could remember. I doubt this is gonna be anything too much for us. You and I been through it. Even if I did come back different, that'd be a blessin'. The fuck either of us got to be happy about in this life?"

"For real, I hear that." Donya threw more of her drink back. "But damn, a half sheet sound like a death wish. You just tryin' to be out for good?"

An uncomfortable silence soon filled the empty warehouse. The crackle of the fire was all I could hear.

Finally, I found the words I was lookin' for. "How long we been at this together? At least about five years, no? Runnin' around these streets like a couple rats. Gettin' our asses beat, dodgin' the cops, livin' off other people's scraps, and whatever chemical escape we can find. And what we got to show for it? What have we come away with?"

Donya shook her head and took another drink. I didn't think she disagreed with me, it just wasn't a nice thought for her to wrap her head around.

"Not much," Donya said.

"So then what we got to look forward to besides gettin' done in by some tweaked-out fiend or freezing to death this winter?"

"Nothin'."

"Right, so I'm gonna take my chances with the half sheet."

"I feel you."

I scratched the side of my face. "So you're with me then?"

Donya grinned, showing her sharp teeth. I always liked it when she smiled. It didn't happen that often, but it made me wanna smile too. She reached into her pocket and pulled out the sheet of acid. It was a big motherfucker. She started to tear it and then looked back up at me. "You know I'm with you, big brother."

I raised my eyebrow, looking into her eyes. "Why you call me that?"

She looked a little embarrassed before she answered. "Call you what?"

"Big brother."

She paused, almost as if she was unsure if she should say what she truly wanted to. Exhaling, her eyes darted to the flames in the barrel, as if she couldn't look me in the eye while she said it.

"Cuz you the only one who ever felt like family to me. I'm grateful for you. If this shit scrambles our brains, I just want you to know, there was at least one person in the world who knew how good you was."

Another awkward silence filled the vacant floor. I wasn't sure how to react.

"Sorry," Donya said, "I know that shit was corny."

"No, it wasn't," I said. "That was real. I'm just trying not to get emotional. That… What you said means a lot to me."

We embraced for a moment, I thought it was just going to be a hug at first, but then she kissed me. I didn't hate it; I just went along with it. It wasn't the first time we'd kissed or even fucked, but something about this kiss felt different. It was more tender, almost loving.

I struggle to describe it now even, but certainly at that point in my life, I didn't know nothin' the likes of such an encounter. But, after about a minute or so, we both stopped and she handed me my half of the sheet.

"I guess I'll see you on the other side," Donya said.

I grinned. "I'm looking forward to it."

UNDER THE INFLUENCE

Harvey Sutton, July 1983

When the shit first hit me, I thought I'd gone blind. The inside of the warehouse went black. It was like someone had put a fuckin' garbage bag over my head. I could hear Donya screaming, soundin' like she was being murdered or somethin'. But I was too melted to move my mouth or even turn my head. I truly thought I was dying.

Eventually, the darkness started to move and grew distinctive hues. It was what I imagine the ocean would look like at midnight. The outline of a cloak manifested, and a featureless figure stood before us.

In my haze, I dubbed him The Dark Man.

Donya's screams suddenly died out, like The Dark Man had control over her body. I still couldn't speak, and my noodle was so fried that I wouldn't have known what to say if I could.

Suddenly, the darkened area behind the figure illuminated. As the murky visual shaped itself, I saw the outline of what looked to be another figure, separate from The Dark Man who was suddenly nowhere to be seen.

"This sick world has molded you into the sadness you embody," a ghostly voice said.

A black mass that made up the second figure started to thin out. Slowly, the dark matter contorted into the outline of a skeleton. The neon green bones glimmered, turning turquoise, before transitioning to white. My eyes squinted when I noticed something in the skeleton's hand. The long spike liquified, changing to a cylindrical body with a point at the end that was familiar to me; it was holding a needle.

Appearing beside the demonic bone body sat a tall cot with a tiny black baby layin' atop it. It was a little girl from the looks of it, but as I continued to study the area, I noticed it wasn't layin' in no ordinary cradle.

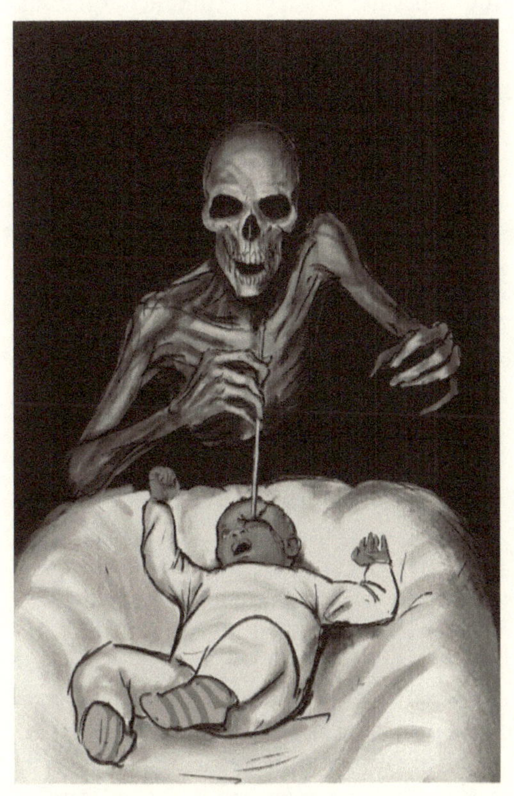

The once mattress-like material turned into a fleshier substance. Curling in on itself, a partially transparent tissue formed, creating an orb of wet meat.

The skeleton grinned like a fiend getting a fix. Pushing the needle and his arm through the gore sphere, the skeleton poked the little girl with the spike, penetrating the suddenly wailing child's eyeball.

My heart raced as a heatwave erupted, making every inch of my body tingle and sweat. What the fuck was that thing doin' to the baby?

I watched the bony hand inject a transparent substance—so much that some of the liquid bubbled outward, causing the girl's eyeball to gush and bug out of her little head.

Donya screamed again. As traumatic as the scene was to me, it was almost like it was even more horrifying to her.

The skeleton then started to bite and slurp the gore bubble. Ingesting the flesh cradle and child in unison. The morbid meal went down the skeleton's throat. Once it arrived in his torso, it began to cling to its bones, forming meat, tendons, and muscle before filling up the anatomical man.

The slick figure grew eyes, nails, skin, nipples, ears, and hair. As it continued to inflate, it shaped out into a middle-aged man with a potbelly. Follicles sprouted from his face and leaped off it. Like a cloud, they hovered, looking like a scribble of angry pen on a sheet of paper. While his identity remained obscured, the clothing that manifested on his body gave me an obvious clue.

The pajama suit covered in blood came with countless stab wounds underneath. A blood-soaked mattress appeared behind him as the pajama man fell backward. The pool of wet crimson sludge atop the brutal bedding splashed and spattered across my face as a wave of weirdness overcame me. A series of sinister giggles echoed throughout the entire warehouse.

I felt my mother's presence.

"It's funny!" she screamed.

I saw her outline manifest on the bed beside my father. The maddening giggles continued to echo. When my mother turned around, her jaw chattered like a nutcracker. She held the knife up to her face, nestling the blade against the corners of her mouth, and continued to cackle.

As the gory blade cut into her facial tissue, she bit down on the steel. She rubbed the blood around her head, circling herself with blurring speed. Her large breasts deflated, and her feminine features morphed into a masculine outline.

The figure was no longer my mother's, and it had become a man. But not just any man; a man who had visited me many nights in the home for displaced boys. I never knew his name, but somehow, he'd known mine.

Plucking the knife from his mouth, vomit started to spew out of his jaws as he unzipped his pants. Enthusiastically, the man began to carve off his genitals. The surge of blood rained over his pants and some of the white meat inside the sex organs became visible.

In a sudden motion, the pervert shoved the bloody bits of his privates into his mouth and chewed. The violent motion of his teeth crushed down onto the slippery organs, forcing the juices to bleed out and dribble down his chin and chest.

"Taste so good!" he roared.

Steaming vomit shot out with his nibbled privates. But as the watery wave connected with the dirt, the man disappeared.

"You grew from the seeds of doom," the disembodied voice from earlier echoed.

The vomit and genitals turned into a melty soup that seeped into the ground, and everything else disappeared. I felt like I was watching a time-lapse in real-time as the plant grew right before my eyes. First it was a seedling, then nearly the size of a small tree. Several branches manifested, each with items appearing that were ready to be picked like ripened apples: a set of glistening balls with a blood-spattered nutsack draped over them; a machine gun with a smoking barrel; a white rock stuffed in a big plastic tube; a gore-slicked sword; a pair of purple high heels; a gas canister; two doves hanging from metal hooks; and a huge can of Spam. A massive steel cage descended over the tree, confining its growth.

"You were both born to fight," the voice continued. "Everyone around you and your-selves. But *never* each other."

As I watched the tree die, a deep feeling of dread came over me. The ground rumbled until a gravestone with the initials B.B. chis-eled upon it was erected with freshly dis-turbed dirt before it.

As the tombstone swelled larger, the font on it sparkled and glistened. I could see the glimmer of diamond rocks embedded within the outline. Below the shine from the stones, the brown dirt was marked with a huge X.

Running out of the darkness, a German Shepard emerged, but this was no ordinary dog. Instead of claws, its paws had human fingers and toes. Slowing near the marking on the dirt, the dog lifted its leg and revealed one more anomaly. As it pissed on the grave, I noticed the stream of yellow pushing through its urethra was coming from a human cock.

"To ascend, you must first build yourself up," the creepy voice continued. "Only then will you be able to board the final ship."

The ground started to rumble again, but this time, like an earthquake. From the grave sprouted countless body parts of all shapes and sizes. Clusters of broken bones and gore topped with a crimson wetness conjoined, forming a display that looked completely unnatural. A clock appeared inside the mass of body parts, only for the white background of the timepiece to begin melting, drizzling a strange white essence all over the dead.

The white liquid formed a specific time: 3:30 AM.

Water suddenly rose from the ground until it surrounded and elevated the pile of mutilated corpses. They all became one, just a sickening glob of violence bobbing in the mini waves. At the top of the gore wad I saw a sparkle—sitting at the pinnacle was a gold throne. When I laid eyes on it, my soul felt inflated. There was nothing I wanted more than to be in that seat.

"Your purpose lies above," the voice said. "The seat is big enough for two."

The first shadowy figure I had seen reappeared. The Dark Man stood in the background, hovering over the mass of gruesomeness and the throne, dwarfing them. I tried to focus, but the static fog overlayed in front of me made what I saw look like poor television reception.

"But you know what you must do," the wicked voice said. "You must do to them what no one else will. The ones who see you as less. The ones who equate you to dirt. You must put them *all* underneath it. Do what you must. It is your *only* purpose. It is your *only* relevance."

That was all I saw on that trip, but then again, at the same time, it wasn't. Outta all my drug experiences, I never seen things repeated before. This one just kept on a loop, showing us the same series of things over and over. It felt like that dark man in the robe—God, Satan, whatever it was—really wanted us to understand the message.

And I read it loud and clear.

When I finally came to, I'd pissed and shit all over myself. I was confused and weakened from losing all my fluids and laying in them—for how many days I don't know. Only thing I did know was that I felt like a changed man. But whether it was for the better or for the worse, I still had no idea.

It wasn't just my physical body where I felt the change, it felt like something more than that. Like the very fuckin' fabric I was crafted from was rewired. I felt the curtain had been pulled back, my eyes were finally open. And there was no way to unsee that shit.

Donya had already awakened lookin' like she'd seen it too. I wanted to ask her if she'd seen the shit I'd seen, but my throat was too dry to talk. She gave me some warm malt liquor, and I was able to finally ask her.

I'd never been more certain of anything in my life: what I'd seen was not only real but an important message.

I felt touched.

Carefully thinking over my approach, I came to the conclusion that I only had one shot at finding out if Donya had been touched too.

We talked for about five or ten minutes, some of what we said is foggy in my memory. But the gist of it is still with me. I know I asked her to tell me what she'd seen. She described some of the *exact* things I'd witnessed. I stopped her a few times and told her several things I'd witnessed that followed what she was revealing in chronological order—some shit she hadn't mentioned yet.

When Donya heard these things, her face looked about as crazy as I'd ever seen it. But there was something else I saw in her expression that I couldn't quite figure. But it would take me years to finally uncover that mystery.

Regardless, at that moment, it was clear—the shit we'd seen was a hundred percent real. Now, I wasn't no scientist—still ain't—but I knew that hallucinations were personal. To have a shared hallucination with another person would be considered supernatural.

But Donya didn't wanna believe what I was saying or what she'd seen with her own goddamn eyes. The whole experience had fucked her up real good.

I tried to reason with her, but before we could finish our discussion, she just took off running. I wanted nothing more than to get up and chase after her, but I was still too weakened from the event.

If I could've told Donya one thing, it would've been that you can run from most anything, except fate.

GRAND THEFT AUTO

Harvey Sutton, December 1984

The car was an '83 Cadillac. Fuckin' thing was a boat. Seein' that my spine was steady aching from crashin' on the concrete entry-ways of the stores, I was attracted to the couch-like seating in the back of the vehicle. But more than anything, I just wanted to be in a warm place for a few hours.

It wasn't the first car I'd broken into, but it was the first one I'd tried to hotwire myself. I traded secrets with some weirdo from the lower east side. Showed him how to hack a payphone to call phone sex lines for free and he showed me how to hotwire a car.

I lied to him, of course. There's no way I knew of to call a sex line for free. I'd just used the remaining minutes on a calling card that I'd lifted from a lady's purse and fluffed up the process with some bogus directions.

I hadn't seen Donya for the better part of a year. Never had I felt so damn alone. The one person who related to me, that I'd spent the last several years with, was gone.

I can't say I blame her. It wasn't like either of us was on the path to success. We were headed down the crapper. While I wasn't happy that she was gone, I hoped she was doing well. I did find myself worrying about her. And without her, I was also worried about myself. Life was getting weird. I was even more lost than before. I felt like a fuckin' zombie.

My head wasn't on a swivel like it had been before. I was gettin' drunk all the time and found myself hooked on a newer drug called crack. I was glad that I'd discovered it—the shit was really gettin' me through. After all the nightmare material that was still burned into my memory, I needed somethin' to zonk me out sometimes.

Whenever I smoked that shit, everything changed. I felt euphoric, almost invincible.

But the fucked up thing was, the feelin' never lasted more than twenty minutes. When I'd first started, it kept on a bit longer. But the more I smoked, the more I noticed the leash kept gettin' shorter.

I probably should've known better, but after I finally got the Caddy started, I blazed inside. As the smoke from the white rock filled the tube, I sucked like I was slurpin' up the best spaghetti I ever had.

The image of a tree walled off by darkness flickered in my head. The white rock and tube dangling from the leaves. I shook it off, trying not to think about it.

For a few minutes, my mind was blown. I was takin' in the shit and my surroundings. Sittin' in that wide, cushy seat that only those fancy fucks get to park their asses on. Feelin' that warm air flow against my cold skin. The shit was heavenly.

But there was one part that wasn't so heavenly. When I smoked rock, thoughts of the tree always resurfaced. That insane night in the warehouse with Donya crept back up. I saw the thing that presented the puzzle and prophecy to us.

I saw The Dark Man.

Donya didn't seem to wanna accept what The Dark Man had told us. Even though she knew that shit was the truth, she just couldn't come to grips with it.

I'd already accepted it. But accepting my truth and committing to it were two completely different things. I'd already subconsciously committed to a life of crime, and that wasn't by choice. Whether I liked it or not, it was my birthright.

But the kind of petty shit I was coastin' through life on wasn't what The Dark Man had envisioned for me. I knew he wanted me to step it up.

I'd thought about it on several occasions: killin' people.

It wasn't the worst idea to come through my head. But the fact that Donya didn't have the same mindset threw me off. Most things we agreed on, but not this. And after that one time we didn't see eye to eye, I'd lost her.

The chain of circumstances only made me wanna act on the commands of The Dark Man even more. I'd been bein' fucked around for my whole life—both figuratively and literally. If there was anyone who had a right to spread the darkness, it was me.

But for some reason, I couldn't get with it. I just drank whatever I could get my hands on, constantly stealing shit to support my crack habit.

I adjusted the rearview mirror and looked into my bloodshot eyes. Once I shivered through the surge of bliss, I got it in my head that I needed to get the car out of the way. As of late, the criminal element in the city was outta control. Fuckin' cops had been *extra* nosy lately.

My plan was to park under this old bridge outside the city—a nice little cozy spot that a lotta people didn't know about. I figured once I got some space between me and the rest of society, I'd have a second to think. What The Dark Man had said was important. If it wasn't, then why would I constantly keep thinkin' about it? I needed to figure out a bigger plan than chasin' my tail in a circle of full-time drug use and petty theft. I felt like I was being swallowed up.

I had a pint of E&J in my pocket that I uncapped when I got the Caddy on the road. But riding all twisted up on brandy and high on crack was a brutal combination, one that I hadn't had any practice at.

There's a lotta things I guess I could've been smarter about in my life, but most people lookin' at this thing would probably say it's pretty obvious that this was the best example.

But most people'd be wrong.

Through the eyes of the unenlightened, this would seem like a terrible mistake. One so severe that it started me on an unimaginable downward spiral. But to me, it's what pivoted my ass toward my destiny.

I was so fuckin' dusted, I never saw that gas station coming.

RAPE & SODOMY

Harvey Sutton, May 1989

They said I should've been dead. As I sat in the jail cell with my bunkmate Rome, often-times, I'd wish that I was.

I'd have figured he'd have gotten sick of fuckin' me up the ass, but he didn't. He put his hand on my thigh.

"Get down here, Crispy," Rome said.

I didn't so much mind suckin' his dick. My jaw got rocked pretty good in the accident, so sometimes when it unhinged it made a weird popping noise. But I'd been suckin' this world's dick since I could remember. What was one more really gonna do?

"Lemme feel that tight shit," Rome said, bending me over the toilet.

Ass up and face on the rim, piss stains and pubic hair clung to the side of my face. That ammonia smell hit hard every time he violated me. The first few times I'd thrown up in the bowl while he was bangin' me, but by this time, I was capable of holding it.

I was getting better at loosening up. He'd dogged me out so many times now my rectum could practically expand on command. Long gone were the days of Slinky prolapses. And in a world where I had little to be grateful for, I was *extremely* grateful.

That particular morning, Rome was going in on me. Whenever he fucked me as hard as he was, it reminded me of the impact of the accident. It was almost on par with it, or, at the very least, the headache I felt after waking up afterward.

They said I hit that fuckin' gas pump at just the right angle. Flames engulfed the entire Cadillac as well as my body. Somehow, doped out of my skull and wired on adrenaline, I was able to scramble outta the car before it blew up. Apparently, the gas station I'd crashed into was also right near the river.

When I hit the water, I put the fire out, but I also passed out. At the very least, I should've drowned. But some good Samaritan had seen the crash and fireball, then jumped in the river and saved me.

Fuckin' cocksucker.

Why couldn't he just let me go? At the time I was pissed he didn't, but looking back, clearly it happened for a reason.

I was chosen.

The shit The Dark Man had said to me before wasn't resonating then, but it was now. When you're trapped in a cage with nothin' but time to think, you start to sort a lotta shit out. Like what's the odds of someone survivin' a double whammy like that gas station barbecue and unconscious river fiasco?

I'm not a numbers guy, but I don't imagine it to be good odds. But you know what has good odds? Coming out of such a situation and lookin' like fuckin' Frankenstein.

In the joint, they nicknamed me Crispy on the count of the 3rd degree burn scars that covered my entire body. At twenty-two years old I wasn't exactly a looker, but at least I still had the aura of a young man. Now, I just looked like a human raisin.

You'd think in the joint that that kind of a look would lend you some credibility, but not me. The inmates sniffed me out in a couple of hours. It wasn't long before I was lookin' like the biggest bitch in the entire facility. The daily punishment I was receiving had me thinkin' about starting to fulfill the request of The Dark Man.

But realistically, no matter how smart I was, there was no way that I was gonna be stackin' bodies inside the cage. That couldn't have been part of the plan.

Best I could figure it was, I'd been spared both physically and legally. I survived the wreck and the system. I'd been in for just about five years with one more on my sentence. If I played it smart, I would be back on the streets soon and free to go wherever the signs swayed me.

I hadn't seen nothin' that I believed to be a sign since I'd been incarcerated, but I still felt somethin'. I hadn't really been looking before, but I was lookin' now. Problem was, ain't much you can look at inside prison. Still, despite my freedom being subdued, I had a feeling. Regardless of what they convict you of, they can't take your feelings from you.

Rome blew his load in my ass and then immediately went to sleep in his bunk. As I sat on the toilet trying to scoop as much cum out of my asshole as possible, I waited for the urge to shit to hit. It was like clockwork, after I got pegged by Rome, he typically knocked somethin' loose.

As I sat on the filthy bowl, I couldn't get my mind off it. That night in the warehouse, the gas station, my uncanny survival—what did it all mean?

It was a miracle that I hadn't killed anyone in the accident. Something that I tried to re-member every time Rome was poundin' my ass in. I had to keep the belief that I was a part of something bigger, not just because that's what I wanted, but because that's what I *needed.*

When one of the guards showed up at our cell a few minutes later, I figured they'd heard us having sex. I was nervous since we get in trouble for that kind of thing. And if we did get caught, Rome always blamed me. And I had to keep my mouth shut and take the heat.

I was relieved to learn that wasn't the rea-son for their presence. Instead, for the first time since I'd been locked up, I had a visitor.

As I was led down to the visiting room, I was racking my brain. Best I could figure it, my lawyer had some paperwork or something. There was no one else I could think of that would have any reason to see me, but I was totally off. There, sitting behind the glass, were eyes filled with sadness.

It was Donya.

I was overwhelmed at first. Almost too shocked to even pick up the phone until she gestured to it.

I felt my lips quiver with hesitation. "I… I thought I'd never see you again."

As I continued to take in her appearance, I realized that it wasn't *just* Donya sitting before me, it was a *new* Donya.

All cleaned up. No more gnarly hair, and no more crazed look. Her posture was so mature and her eyes, while glossed over, were also filled with care.

"I know… I'm sorry, Harv," she replied.

Tears started rolling down her cheeks when she saw the severity of my scars. It was hitting her hard. I must've looked like a monster. Seeing her all emotional upset me inside.

"You don't gotta apologize," I said. "You ain't done nothing wrong."

She did her best to compose herself, swallowing her emotions like a shot of harsh gin. As I watched her wiping her eyes, I decided to change the subject.

"So, what brings you here?" I asked.

Donya did her best to shake it off and try to control her sobbing. "I-I heard about what happened to you."

"Really? How?"

"You blew up a gas station… A lotta people heard about it."

"Oh."

She furrowed her brow. "You know, it took me a really long time to even have the guts to come up here. I'm still not sure if it was the right choice."

"W-why wouldn't it be the right choice?"

"Because, as much as I cared—" Donya quickly corrected herself, "care about you, we were really fuckin' bad for each other. That last shit we did in the warehouse… after that, I knew I had to change my life."

I stayed quiet for a moment. I knew just letting her talk would be best. She'd clearly come to the prison because she needed to get something off her chest. If I pushed her early, I might never find out what.

I had few forms of entertainment outside of my own curiosity. Scratching the side of my face, I listened.

"And ever since that night," Donya continued, "things have been better for me. Not great, but at least better."

"I'm really happy to hear that," I replied. "It's somethin' that I've always found myself wondering about—if you was in a decent spot. It's what I was hopin'."

"Thanks."

I wasn't quite sure where to go from there, so I asked her what anyone would. "So, what have you been up to?"

"I, ah, I got a job, and an apartment now. I just work and try to keep my nose clean. How about you?"

I made a face that screamed *yikes*. "Well, before this became my new home, I had a bit of a drug problem. But since I came in here, I been clean a few years now, and I'm back on the level."

"That's good," Donya said. "It'll be easier for you to keep your shit together with your head clean."

"Yeah. I only got maybe a year left until my sentence is up, then I should be..."

I stopped dead in my tracks. The television in the visiting room had a big enough screen for me to just be able to view the picture. I saw news footage of what looked to be a gravesite with a bold headline ribbon on the bottom of the screen that read: B.B. Services Held Today.

Images from that night in the warehouse erupted in my mind. It was too accurate to be a coincidence. The only time I'd ever seen a gravestone with the letters 'B.B.' was when The Dark Man showed me and Donya. Then suddenly, she returns out of nowhere and the headline on the screen behind her shows a grave with the *exact* same lettering. It was too specific to be a coincidence.

"Turn around, quick!" I said, pointing.

Donya looked at me like I was crazy but humored my request. When she looked at the screen, what she saw didn't trigger a reaction.

"On the TV, do you see it?" I asked.

"Yeah, I see it. It's sad and all, but what does a washed-up pop star have to do with anything?"

"Huh? In case you forgot, I'm in prison. I have no fuckin' idea what's happenin' outside these walls."

"The initials stand for Bianca Blush, the local girl with the 'Make you Blush' jam," Donya said. "She switched to initials. You know her, she was a big deal when we were kids. Not so much anymore. I guess she overdosed on some pills or somethin'."

My eyes widened. "It's like that night."

"What are you talking about?"

"What we saw together, inside the warehouse."

Shaking her head, Donya returned her gaze to me. "I-I don't know about any of that shit, man."

"What do you mean? That was part of it, we-we talked about it after we came back through. We shared the same hallucination, only it wasn't a hallucination. It was real."

"No!" Donya slammed her open hand down. "I didn't come here to talk about all the times we got fucked up, okay! I came here to show you that you can change. That you don't have to keep hurtin' if you're strong enough."

It wasn't until that moment when she shook her head in frustration that I noticed her tiny earrings. Silver doves of hope hanging from each earlobe.

I pictured the bizarre tree The Dark Man revealed to us with countless random items hanging from it. Were *we* the doves? Was our destiny awaiting us?

"But it's the truth, Donya. We both saw the exact same shit! And just like the tree showed us, you've got—"

"Stop! The truth is, after that fuckin' night, we was both traumatized. We each went off on our own separate way. The shit I seen scared me straight. I'm grateful I seen what I seen, but that don't make it real. If nothin' else, that shit made me realize there's no way I'm ever gonna let myself fall back into all the darkness again." She got up from her seat. "But it did just the opposite for you. It pushed you over the edge."

I looked at her calmly but like I was staring into her soul. In some ways, I felt I was. We were the doves of destiny. We could fight with the world and even with ourselves, but never with each other. Donya would eventually realize that.

"The signs are there," I said. "You may not want to admit it, but as time goes on, you'll see. You and I weren't put here to work a job and have an apartment."

"Then what was we put here for?" Donya screamed.

I kept my cool, eyes fixed on hers. "You know what we was put here for."

Another tear welled up in Donya's eye and beaded down her face. She hunched over sideways preparing to set the phone on the hook. But before she did, she managed what her emotions had been holding back. What I imagine were the most difficult words we ever exchanged.

"Goodbye, big brother," she whispered.

GRAVE ROBBERY

Harvey Sutton, March 1990

I left prison in some clothing that was purchased for me by the state. Pretty lame threads, nothing I would've chosen, but what was I gonna do? After the gas station explosion, they'd cut off all the burned stuff in the emergency room.

Standing at the barbwire fence, I wasn't sure if I was ready to insert myself back into the world again. All I had to my name was my clothes, twenty dollars of gate money, and a single cab ride to wherever I wanted. But I did have something else I suppose. Something that wasn't plainly visible.

A plan.

Staring at the yellow cab and the pale man smoking inside it, I knew *exactly* where I was going. I hadn't gotten any other visits from Donya since she walked out on me. In fact, she was the last—and only—person from the outside that I interacted with until my sentence was finally complete. But I never forgot our talk, those silver doves dangling from her ears, or what I saw on the television screen. She might not've realized it, but eventually, she would. She had to. That's the thing about fate, it doesn't leave you with a choice.

"Where ya headed?" the driver asked as I pulled on the handle.

"Landry's Hardware," I said, hopping inside the car.

The cabbie took another deep pull of his smoke and raised his eyebrow. I could tell he was repulsed by my burns. I was grateful I hadn't lost all my hair in the gas station explosion, but the patchiness of the growth made me look uncomfortably weird. It was better than nothin', I guess.

"The hardware store?" the cabbie asked. "That's where you wanna go?"

"Yeah."

The guy shook his head but didn't ask me any more questions. When we arrived at the hardware store, I got out of the car, and he left me. I was officially on my own, and it felt damn good.

I was excited but a little nervous too. What I'd been thinking about for nearly a year in the joint was finally gonna happen.

Inside the store, I was able to find a small shovel for a few dollars. I would still need a way to conceal it though. Since I was on foot, I didn't want to draw attention to myself walking around with a shovel. It's an odd look for a guy fresh out.

I ended up grabbing a duffel bag to hide the shovel inside of. When I cashed out, I felt like I had everything I needed.

The reason I'd picked Landry's Hardware was because it was close to St. Ann Cemetery. Walking didn't take me long, but I still had a lot of questions floating around in my head. I didn't have doubts or anything; I was as confident as a juiced-up prize fighter. But there's always gonna be stuff that makes you wonder. The older I got, the more I realized such things. I'd probably spent the better part of my life questioning my purpose.

Thankfully, I was ready to get on with things. Given the earliness of the year, I was expecting a tougher dig. But with that March having been so unusually warm, the ground had softened. That wasn't just some stroke of luck, it was a sign that I was on the right path.

It wasn't some coincidence that Bianca Blush had been buried in her hometown either. Finding her grave was easy enough, but digging it up took a while. I had to wait until it got dark. After several hours, when I finally struck the top of the casket, I couldn't have been more eager to see what was inside.

The vision I'd had finally brought me to where I needed to be. The diamond font wasn't on the gravestone, but I'm no dummy. That was obviously symbolic. The X on the grave plot was telling me there was probably some kind of valuable object buried *with* her. That's what I believed anyhow.

It took a bit more work, but when I got the coffin cracked open, sadly, that wasn't the case. Bianca was buried in a ratty-ass dress and a pair of scuffed high heels. It was quite shocking. The image of the girl I remembered on the cover of the magazines had faded. And there wasn't no jewelry, no items, no nothin'.

I slumped down on the ground, dumb-founded. There wasn't much going through my mind, and I was starting to panic. I grabbed at the sides of my head, pulling at my hair like a mad-man. What if I was wrong? What if what I'd seen all those years ago in the warehouse was wrong? Was I just overanalyzing and trying to position a string of coincidences to give myself hope?

I recalled the memory of Donya dressed all proper sitting in front of me in prison. She had her shit together. She had a plan.

What did I have now?

I couldn't help but wonder if she was right. Then, like a bolt of lightning from God, it hit me: the X on the grave wasn't to sym-bolize some kind of prize. Her plot wasn't a fuckin' box of cereal. No, it wasn't about Bianca being buried with something of value. It was Bianca *herself* who held the value.

NECROPHILIA

Harvey Sutton, June 1990

I stood under the bridge looking at Bianca's decaying body. It was warming up and the insects were really starting to do a number on the broad. It was almost like a full-time job keeping them at bay.

Looking back at the car, the blindfolded bum was glowing with excitement. Despite it being warm outside he was still dressed in his winter clothes, sweatin' like a true weirdo. It had taken me many years, but I'd finally made it to the spot I was trying to reach the night of the crash. But this time around, I'd learned my lesson. When I stole *this* Cadillac, I wasn't high on crack or drunk. I was only focused on the task at hand.

There was still a bit of pressure involved though. Knowing that I needed to remember how to steal a car, get back to Bianca's dugout grave, and remove her body before sunrise was a tall task. But it all came together. I wasn't surprised in the slightest. And it didn't come together because I got lucky. It came together because I had done just as The Dark Man had told me to.

But there was one thing I was *definitely* wrong about…

If I was going to harm enough of the ones who'd wronged me—the amount throbbing inside that bloody jumble of bodies I saw back at the warehouse—then I was gonna need some money. Sure, I could kill a guy here and a girl there, but what was that really gonna do?

I approached the passenger side door of my hot Caddy. Stolen or not, she still looked pretty. The bum was grinning. Only a few of his teeth weren't rotted out of his mouth.

I could've easily killed the fuckin' bum right then. I even thought about it. But I reminded myself killing a few wasn't gonna get me far. It would most likely just land me back upstate—maybe for good this time.

No, that wasn't a part of the puzzle that The Dark Man had put in front of me. I needed to build my way up to a much larger event. Something that was going to get me a major body count in a single shot.

But in the meantime, I had to figure out the puzzle. At that time, my best guess was that Bianca's body was the key. I figured after the corpse went missin' that, eventually, the family would offer some kind of reward for some information. Surely they would want their loved one to be at peace. Surely they wouldn't rest until she was.

The plan was great. What's better than holdin' someone for ransom? Holdin' a dead body for ransom. There's no maintenance or upkeep—aside from keepin' the ants off her ass—*and,* if I somehow got caught, the jail time would be minimal in comparison.

Only problem was, so far, nothing of the sort had transpired. I'd been checking the papers and tabloids religiously. There were a couple of articles printed about her after I snatched her, but soon after, no one seemed to care.

I guided the homeless man out of the car until we were under the bridge. It was just a concrete wall, bushes, and Bianca's body.

"Wow, I never seen no celebrity before," the bum said. "It's her. It's really fuckin' her."

"Course it's really her," I said.

In the meantime, until I figured out the ransom situation, I'd found a few weirdos who were interested in seeing her. Guys too whacked out for me to be worried about the cops believing. I told 'em in advance that they'd have to be blindfolded beforehand if they wanted to fuck her.

I didn't want none of these bastards coming back and double-dipping, or worse, to be able to tell the cops where she was if they somehow got a conscience.

"What happened to her shoulder?" the guy asked.

"Dunno," I said. "Raccoon might've got into her or something."

The tissue there was starting to fall apart, and on top of it, some kind of pest had taken several other bites out of her. I looked at the folded tarp that I used to keep her covered when I wasn't there. Maybe I just needed to start wrapping her up tighter.

At this rate, she wasn't gonna be my cash cow for long. The face—her most important feature—was thankfully still intact.

That was the major thing. It's what the guys needed to verify that it was actually her and know they weren't gettin' stiffed.

"Gimmie the money," I said.

The bum forked over the ten dollars and I gave him a few moments of privacy. I could hear him fuckin' her and yelling at her. If you ask me, the tone he'd taken was unnecessary. Some tough guy shit. Kinda pathetic, the old loon tryin' to be tough with a dead broad.

"Fuckin' bitch," the guy said, slamming his dirty dick inside her. "You like makin' them little songs, don't you, cunt? You make 'em for me, bitch? Ain't that right?"

It went on like that, him scolding a corpse for making music. I could also hear him slapping her around a bit.

"Hey, asshole, no hittin' her," I said.

"Alright, alright."

I couldn't have the guy haulin' off and damagin' my goods. It wasn't uncommon. Some guys got a little too excited. But it was my job to keep 'em in check.

I didn't really like the way he treated Bianca. Actually, I didn't really like the way any of the guys did. I felt different about her than they did.

I remembered the stories I'd heard about how she was a tough kid from the streets. Not just the streets, but our streets. Those fuckers should show a little more respect for her. She wasn't one of those Hollywood-type cunts until she'd actually become one.

Those upscale types were the ones I wanted to offer up to The Dark Man. But not Bianca, she was different than them. I felt the need, as I so often did, to remind her.

"Hey buddy, I heard you cum," I said. "Time's up."

"But I went kinda quick," he whined. "I was hopin' for a round two. You know, really make this count."

"You can have round two when you get your hands on another ten bucks. But right now, you need to put your dick in your pants and that blindfold back on. Don't fuckin' test me, understood?"

Pulling the butterfly knife out of my pocket, I looked that son-of-a-bitch in the eyes. I was just lookin' for a reason to poke 'em. I didn't flip it open, but I did make him aware that I had it. With a bit of money coming in, thanks to Bianca, I had some means of protecting my investment.

I dropped the guy off in a park about ten minutes away and returned to Bianca's body as quickly as possible. I liked fuckin' her after the other guys had just cum inside her—it was the best. That way, when we made love, the warmth of their sperms on my cock made it feel like she was still alive.

"You're better than the way he treated you," I whispered, not wanting to just stick it in her. After the way the homeless guy had acted, she deserved a little romance.

Nobody cared about her enough to want to know where she was. They all just used her up. In that way, we had somethin' in common. The world had used us both up.

"I appreciate you," I whispered, inserting my throbbing cock into her oily cunt. I was severely disappointed when I couldn't feel any of the bum's hot cum.

I used my hand to shoo away a cluster of flies that were swirling around her rotting scalp. An off-white sludge oozed not only from her eyeballs but also her earlobes. I brushed a cluster of ants off her tit before flipping her on her side to get better access to her holes. I bent her rotten legs back, being careful not to rip one off.

"He must'a cum in her fuckin' ass instead," I grumbled.

I'd only fucked her in the ass a few times before, but it brought back a lot of bad memories. I didn't like thinkin' about assholes gettin' pushed in.

While I was makin' love to Bianca, I was forced to think about the joint, and Rome reamin' me out. Shit was weird, and not in an enjoyable way. But her asshole was where it was wet and warm, so I was willing to make my trauma a part of my fantasy. At least I was the one doing the fuckin' this time around.

When I pulled my cock out of Bianca's pussy, a small amount of green muck flowed from her. A big cluster of dead black ants were congealed together by the slime. Slappin' the sludge aside, I nestled my mushroom tip into her rotten rectum. I'm not sure what was different this time, maybe the flesh had been out in the heat for too long after being stretched, but it had retracted in on itself.

The tightness and seeing the dribble of cum leaking out her ring made me want to get inside so bad. Every time I fucked her, I felt like I was fuckin' a supermodel. Or, as she further decayed, at the very least, the mother of one.

"I always thought you were beautiful," I said, sweet-talkin' her. "When I seen you on the magazine covers as a kid, you were always the prettiest. Just because no one else wants you, doesn't mean I don't."

I picked up the cluster of green gunk and dead ants, and fingered some of it into her asshole, tryin' my best to warm it up. After a few minutes of repetition, I had my cock balls deep. The guy's cum wasn't hot anymore, but it was still kinda warm. It didn't take long for me to add to it.

PROSTITUTION

Harvey Sutton, August 1990

I stood out on the street, trying to look sexy. It was a tough sell for guy who'd been nicknamed Crispy. But every doorknob gets a turn. For each freak like me, there was someone waiting. Multiple people, surprisingly.

The job market wasn't callin' for fresh felons. My deep-fried face didn't exactly look like one you could trust. Pity, maybe. But pity can only get a guy so far. Sometimes I'd start thinkin' that maybe all that stuff I saw in the warehouse was mumbo jumbo. But deep down, I knew there was an undeniable plan. There had to be.

Still, if there was, I'd have to fuckin' survive to see it. So after Bianca's body had rotted to a point where it was no longer recognizable and lost all value, I was forced to figure somethin' out.

With my only means of income having been spoiled, I got to thinkin'. After gettin' my ass fucked against my will in the joint, peddling it didn't feel so weird. I ain't a faggot or nothin', but sometimes you just gotta figure somethin' out.

I noticed most of the clientele were older guys. They normally wanted blowjobs in their cars, so I didn't have to do too much anal. I was relieved when I recognized the older guy that pulled up to me.

I'd been with him before.

The guy, Rodger, as he'd introduced himself, was well-spoken. His luxury car, slick clothing, fancy watch, and overall cleanliness made him seem like he was well off. It always seemed a bit odd to me that he would be in such an area. I figured he was probably married, one of those closeted queer types. One time, when he slid his pants off, he was wearing women's lingerie. Rodger was a cross-dressin' queer at the very least.

I took comfort in knowing that this wasn't my first time with him. There was nothing worse than getting into a creepy car with an absolute stranger. It made you wonder if you'd even be gettin' out. But this time, when I got inside, things were different.

Rodger wasn't so to the point and didn't treat me like a piece of meat. It was less transactional, and he seemed legit interested in me as a person. This was obvious because the first thing he asked me had nothing to do with sex.

"I don't know if I quite remember your name since the last time," he said. "Would you care to remind me?"

"It's Harvey," I said. "But why do you even care?"

"Because, I think you have potential. I believed it the first time we met."

"Potential as what?" I raised my eyebrow. "A deep-fried crackhead?"

"I didn't—"

"Listen, you'll have to forgive my hesitation," I interrupted. "But there ain't a lot of people in this world that've said those words to me. You're out on a fuckin' limb with that one, bud."

"Those without a carefully trained eye will not see a diamond in the rough. But I see you, Harvey. Not only do I see you, but I'd like to help you."

The word diamond rang in my head when he said it. It made me think of glittery lettering on the trippy version of Bianca's grave. Since things had fell through with me holding the pop star's corpse for ransom, I hadn't thought a whole lot about what The Dark Man had asked of me. I was more focused on survival. If I was being honest with myself, I was on the fence. My faith in the warehouse vision continued to flip-flop. Did I really believe it? I'd been pushing hard to get to a point where I could do some real damage, however, nothing ever seemed to come of it.

Maybe the hallucination was just that.

Part of me wondered if this was a turning point. Were things about to shake out for me the way they had for Donya? She'd moved on from the events of that night at the warehouse, and maybe it was time for me to do the same. I found myself in a unique position: I could follow the signs *and* look to turn things around with the same choice.

"How so?" I asked.

"I think if I cleaned you up a bit, that you could be a lot of help to me," Rodger said. "But, before we explore your potential, we must see if you actually have any. What do you say, old friend?"

I didn't have a whole lot going on besides stealin' and whorin'. Even though I had no idea what he saw in me, I'd have been a fool to say no. I slowly nodded.

"Wait," I raised my eyebrow, "does this mean I still have to suck your cock?"

Rodger didn't answer me. He just unzipped his pants.

FALSE IMPRISONMENT

Harvey Sutton, January 1991

I gazed down at my reflection inside the chrome bowl. Somehow, I didn't look like a total piece of shit anymore. But I felt like one. Still, I couldn't deny how fuckin' amazing I looked. My eyes darted to the other dish filled with nuggets and jelly-like gravy, then back to my reflection.

The burns that once made me look like a strewn-together quilt of a man were no more. I did look a bit like a plastic surgery template, but the burns were gone. Along with the skin transplant came a hair transplant. It seemed like there were no lengths he wouldn't go to.

Rodger had even had a few of the teeth that had rotted or gotten knocked out of my mouth replaced with pearly fake ones. He also had the rest of my teeth cleaned and whitened, my hair cut and styled, and my skin tanned until I transitioned from a pasty white boy to a beautiful bronze stallion.

I was a new man.

I looked better than I ever did before. He had me on a strict diet, not exactly the type of food I would've preferred, but it was clean and well-seasoned, until recently…

In addition to the physical modifications, and nutritional changes, Rodger also had me working out regularly. There were so many good things happening for me that it was hard to keep track of them all. I felt beyond blessed, and for my new lavish lifestyle, I hadn't paid a cent. But that didn't mean that it didn't cost me anything.

I moved around in the cage, trying my best to work my way into a position I didn't hate. But I was naked and the floor had been getting so cold lately that it didn't seem possible to get comfortable. I missed the soft bounce of the mattress and warmth of the comforter and silk sheets.

Rodger was responsible for my metamorphosis. He referred me to his doctors, let me stay at his house, and use his personal chefs and athletic trainer. After a few months of healing, eating, and exercise, I officially didn't recognize the guy in the mirror. The reflection I saw was one of the people I used to loathe. But now that I was one of them, I didn't feel that hatred any longer. I wondered if that was how Donya had felt sitting in front of me in the visitation space.

Everything was going perfectly until one evening during dinner, I passed out while eating. The best that I could figure was Rodger had the chef put some horse tranquilizer in my dinner.

When I woke up, I was inside the kennel. I'd been forced to walk on all fours ever since that time. Rodger treated me like a goddamn dog, not only in how he spoke to me, what he fed me, and where he kept me, but also by the 'tricks' he taught me.

I'd spent nearly two full months, morning, noon, and night, doing tricks for that fuck. Fetching, running obstacle courses, and practicing my gait and posture. It was pure insanity.

At the end of my early dog days, my knees would be all torn up and my hands and elbows would ache. My body wasn't used to such positioning.

If I got upset or tried to speak out at all, I got whipped or electrocuted with a cattle prod. Rodger always had several armed men at his disposal, so there was never a chance for me to fight back or escape.

Throughout all the prep, he continued to talk about 'the show.' That was what we'd been preparing for the entire time. I had no idea what the show was or what it meant. But as I waited in my kennel, I had a terrible feeling worming through my insides.

How could I not have a bad feeling?

I messed up several weeks back when trying to jump a small hurdle on his custom course while keeping pace with him. After that screwup, unlike other times, he said nothing to me.

Later that night, I awoke to violence. Two men pulled me out of the cage and pinned me to the floor. Rodger watched as a third man used a scalpel to splice open my nutsack. Crudely, the man reached inside, yanking. My cries did nothing to stall him.

When he yanked my testicles out of their protective layer, the blood vessels and sperm ducts grew tense. It felt like someone was pulling on my soul.

"This one can't listen properly," Rodger had said. "I suppose allowing him to breed would be a foolish decision."

The blood sprayed as my cords were cut. They only put me out after neutering me. Rodger wanted me to feel it. I woke up in a puddle of my own blood with a couple dozen stitches in me, closing up the hole my balls had been ripped out of.

They used a pressure washer to hose me down the next morning. I haven't felt the same since. There's something missing inside me, and I don't mean my nuts or pride. It's something else that goes even deeper. While I don't know what it is exactly, I'll tell you this: after that shit, I never fucked up another trick. I've been flawless.

I continued to stare at my food dish, eyes darting to the door hopelessly. That bastard should've been there already. Had something changed? Had 'the show' been canceled? Then, the door sprung open, and Rodger stood with two of his men.

"Come, come now," Rodger said to his men. "We're already running late. But remember, be especially careful with him today during transportation. I need him in prime condition. Not a hair out of place."

The men agreed, placing my kennel onto a square dolly before wrapping a black sheet over the entire thing. I listened closely as I was loaded onto what I believe to be a truck, transported, then unloaded.

The cloth placed over my cage had a small tear in it. Through the hole, I saw many more cages and heard barking. But the barking wasn't a sound like a dog would make, it was off in tone, like nothing I'd ever heard. It sounded both animalistic and human at the same time.

A short time later the veil was ripped off, revealing Rodger standing outside my cage holding what looked like a dog collar. But the collar in his wrinkly hands was no normal choker. It was made of white gold and studded with countless diamonds.

"Now, my boy, I bestow to you what you've earned," Rodger whispered. "You're not perfect, but for what you are, you reached your potential faster than I could've hoped."

He looked almost tearful when he fastened the collar around my neck and clipped on the leash. I watched him reach into his pocket and pull out a mint.

I started to pant, knowing from past experience that he would've been upset if I didn't act thrilled by the reveal of the 'treat.' Rushing up to his hand, I lapped at the Life Savers Wint-O-Green and took it into my mouth. As I sucked upon it, I sought his praise, nestling the top of my head against his fingers while discreetly using my hand to scratch where my balls should have dangled. My sack skin had never healed quite right—it was always extra itchy.

"Don't be stupid!" Rodger yelled. "You'll make a mess of your hair."

I calmed myself, posturing down and letting out a little whimper. He usually liked it when I did that.

"I've worked long and hard with you at this," Rodger said. "Do *not* disappoint me."

I panted quietly to signify my obedience.

"Let's go then."

Rodger led me past all the other cages into a hallway. A pair of men wearing tuxedos opened the doors for us.

"Posture," Rodger reminded me.

I tried to strut into the room as proudly as I could, showing off my toned physique and whitened teeth. I didn't give them too much tongue, just a bit of panting like we'd game-planned.

The space itself was massive, but the audience was limited. A panel of four judges sat with scorecards and pencils in hand. The fifth stood at the end of the table, waiting.

Erected across from the scorekeepers sat a few fancy, padded bleachers. Several dozen wealthy-looking types watched sipping on their elegant cocktails. One woman looked through a pair of obnoxiously small binoculars. Beside her sat a shriveled, older man who looked giddy.

They were insane.

Every last one of them.

"Come," Rodger commanded.

Rodger first led me to the standing judge. The man in the suit couldn't have been more pleased to inspect me. With the twinkle in his eye, you'd have thought he was squeezin' on some monster tits or somethin'. Grabbing at my chin, he used his fingers to maneuver my lips around until they were spread to his liking. It seemed that he was checkin' my teeth and gums out.

He then squatted over me, feeling my biceps, ass, and thighs. After moving on from my muscles, he ran his fingers through my coat, examining my hair, before spending some time caressing my deflated nutsack. I could hear him whispering something under his breath, but I couldn't hear what.

I wasn't expecting him to slap me across the face, but when he did, I wasn't upset. Rodger had conditioned me during our sessions with the stun gun and whip. I never fought back, I just stood firm. Plus, I was completely emasculated—I literally had no balls anymore.

Rodger's eyes gleamed when I didn't flinch. I knew I'd done well, and he was pleased with my reaction.

"Off!" the man yelled.

Rodger snapped his head in my direction. "Come, Harvey!"

To wrap things up, Rodger paraded me around the entire space, and I jumped over various objects. I did some cone drills, weaving in and out, ran through a few tires, and searched for a few items inside a sandbox. I believe I found them quicker than expected. I kept pace with Rodger for the entire event, knowing that's what he expected of me.

A handful of the old weirdos watching from the stands clapped excitedly, so I figured I must've done well enough. After the run we waited in the back, watching all the other human dogs come out one by one.

It was a short time after the last demonstration that Rodger and I were called back out. The massive banner hanging above the stage read: The Human Dog Show XXVI.

I can't say I was surprised when they pinned that blue, 'best in show' ribbon to my cheek. I'd earned it. But I couldn't help but wonder, with the human dog show over, what did Rodger have in store for me next?

ROBBERY & MURDER

Harvey Sutton, January 1991

Later that evening, I was brought back home and led into a study that I'd never been inside before. Several armed men left Rodger and me at the doors before closing them. Our late-night celebration was about to begin.

Rodger sat down on the couch. He unclipped my leash, while I waited for his command on all fours.

"You know," he said, "you've really made me proud. I couldn't have done any of this without you."

When I looked into his eyes I could see the fire of pride burning.

Getting up from the couch, Rodger removed the 'best in show' ribbon from his pocket and approached the mantle. When he pinned it to a rectangle of corkboard, I noticed it was resting beside several others.

Seeing the additional ribbons immediately unsettled me. Who had won those awards? And, more importantly, where the fuck were they now? A grave feeling came over me, followed by a supreme sense of urgency.

"You know," Rodger said, "one can have many unique objects. My collection is quite extensive." He pointed to a painting on the wall. "This is a Monroe."

I tried my best to look excited, perking up as I continued to listen to him speak.

"It's a one-of-a-kind portrait of a French nobleman that dates back to 1649. The funny thing about the gentleman depicted here is, he believed that eating his own sperm would not only get him pregnant, but eventually make him immortal."

I bit my lip, unsure where he was going with his weird little talk.

"Of course we know that's not how nature works." Rodger chuckled. "No, he was just another fucking creep with a fetish."

It was ironic coming from Rodger, the biggest fuckin' creep I knew.

"Or take, for example, this lion's head. That very beast was responsible for devouring twenty-six men over a single summer in Kenya. It's like having a serial killer's head hanging on your wall."

The taxidermized lion's head suspended several yards away was intimidating. I imagined the animal's claws and teeth ripping into men and pulling them apart. That'd be a tough way to go.

Rodger then gestured back to the fireplace mantle. Above the glow of the flames hung a silver sword that glimmered in the dim lighting.

"But this piece…" Rodger said. "This took far more lives than that lion. Three hundred and eight to be exact."

I instantly wondered if it was by his hand or someone else's. He didn't mention any specific time period or other historical tidbits along with it like he had for the other pieces. The absence of information filled me with unease.

"Do you know what the secret to this item's effectiveness is?" Rodger asked.

I shook my head.

"It's the weight. Most swords are cumbersome. But this one, while just as deadly as the rest, is no more difficult than holding a cane." His eyes twinkled. "Maybe I'll give you a little demonstration later."

Rodger returned his gaze back to the row of awards lining the mantle. My pubic region suddenly ached. I hadn't noticed it initially, but there, above the awards, sat a jar filled with yellow liquid that my testicles were floating inside of. The anger within me flared. My manhood was merely another trinket to the fuckin' bastard. The whispers of The Dark Man hummed in my eardrums.

"But these…" Rodger seemed to get a bit emotional at the sight of the awards. "These mean far more than any of the objects I just told you about. Why, you ask? Because I didn't buy these." Rodger reached out, stroking the ribbon tenderly like it was a child's face. "I earned them."

I'd been around the man long enough to realize he was insane. The truth was, I had no idea what this fuckin' guy was gonna do next. But when he turned away from the fireplace and opened a cabinet to reveal a bottle of scotch and a jar of peanut butter, it became very obvious.

He threw back nearly an entire glass in two gulps before setting himself up with another. As Rodger opened the peanut butter, I could see the erection growing in his pants. Dropping his drawers, he plunged his pecker deep into the Jif. I knew what he was going to have me do next.

I'm not sure if it was because he was talking about all the death beforehand, but suddenly, the vision from the warehouse returned. I'd been trying not to think about it so much, the hallucination had never done much good for me. In reality, it could've been what fueled my downward spiral.

But when I recalled the part of the trip when the man cut off his own genitals and ate them, I shuddered. The pair of testicles hanging on the tree flashed in my mind and my eyes immediately darted to the jar with my testicles in it.

Enough was enough. That son-of-a-bitch had clipped my nuts and put them on his fireplace like a knickknack. I couldn't let that just be the end of it. If I did, then he would've had every right to emasculate me. I didn't care what the repercussions were, I'd sucked Rodger's cock for the last time.

I'd been practicing my gait for months, so it wasn't difficult for me to move around quietly. But when I stood up, my legs were a little wobbly from lack of use. Once I straightened out my knees, I was able to find my footing. It was only the clanging of the metal as I lifted the sword off the mantle that finally alerted him.

"W-what are you doing?!" Rodger asked. "Bad! Get down!" His eyes widened with horror when he realized I was done takin' orders.

My heart was thrashing in my chest like a cat stuck in a blanket as I raised the sword. I felt sick to my stomach. Was I really capable of taking another life?

What felt like a consolidation of my hatred, anger, and depression swirled like a vicious whirlpool inside me. The Dark Man lived. With his energy and my own, I had answered my own question.

"Get down!" Rodger screamed.

"It's time for you to get down," I said. "Under the fuckin' dirt."

He was right about the sword. It felt like I was swingin' a whiffle ball bat. And the thing was even sharper than it looked. I made the first slash across his throat.

The massive slash sprayed blood all over the cabinet behind him. Rodger immediately clasped at his throat while his tongue flailed around his mouth like a fish out of water.

I circled sideways, bringing the next slice upward, aiming for his arm. Along the way, I cut off the tip of his peanut-butter-dipped pecker before driving the blade up through his armpit and shoulder.

Rodger fell to the ground, bleeding profusely and twitching. I could see his arm bone along with the meat and muscle around it. He looked like one of those old cartoon drawings for a second. The gashes were so deep that he was going to be out of his misery in just a short time. *Lucky bastard.* After what he'd put me through, he deserved worse. I needed to leave him with the final act of degradation that he deserved.

I looked up at the mantle, where my testicles were floating. Twisting off the cap of the semi-clouded jar, I retrieved my boys. The scent of the alcohol he'd used to preserve them stung my nostrils. I looked down at the gaping wound across his throat and took a knee. I slid my nuts into his mouth and listened to him choke.

"You wanted 'em so bad," I said. "Well, now they're yours."

The roles had been reversed. It was now Rodger who was gagging on my body. As I watched him struggle to gasp for air, I poured the alcohol brine into his open throat wound. He kicked and cried like a manic child, but that didn't stop me from dumping the rest onto the flat slice at the end of his cock.

I waited nearly another hour inside the study with Rodger's corpse. The men who'd brought us inside were armed, and one of the first things I learned on the streets was never bring a knife to a gunfight. I was at a disadvantage, but the one thing I did have on my side was the element of surprise. If used properly, it could be a powerful asset.

The feeling of taking another life had struck me—the emotions came in waves. I threw up. Knowing Rodger was a sick bastard made it somewhat easier than how I imagined killing a stranger might feel, but in a lot of ways, he was the only guy that ever did shit for me. Even though he'd helped me for selfish reasons, he'd still helped me. For a while, it just felt like having the father I never had, minus all the cock suckin'.

I think that was the part that made me vomit and kind of feel depressed at first. Despite all the terrible things I'd done and aspired to do, actually killing someone was a whole different ball game. And after the bad vibes wore off, I was left to taste the flavor of murder at its core.

It was sweeter than I expected.

Maybe that's because my taste buds had grown accustomed to the salty. But nothing came close to what I was feeling. It was a high I couldn't get from a crack pipe and much different than any of the times I'd done LSD.

I'd been regulated to a submissive role for the last several months and even stretching back to my time in prison. I'd grown so accustomed to being a human bitch that it was only fitting Rodger had turned me into one. But after killing him, I realized that I was done being *anyone's* bitch.

Outside of the strange euphoria bubbling in my chest and brain, I also suddenly felt like I finally had a purpose again. While I hadn't planned for the murder to snap my mindset back into The Dark Man's commands, it had. But I knew that to accomplish what I'd been offered, this was only the beginning.

I readied myself by the door, and eventually, as I suspected, one of Rodger's guards returned to check on us. When that handle turned, I was ready.

"Mr. M—"

Before he could get the words out, I'd plunged my blade into his belly. I twisted and drove it upward, creating a wide gash from his pelvis to the bottom of his ribcage.

His hand went limp, and his Uzi fell onto the floor. I tossed him onto the carpet, retracting the sword from his innards. The man landed on his back, trying to scream but instead coughed up ropes of dark blood.

As I raised the sword a second time, he raised his hands. The steel cut through several of his fingers before connecting with his forehead. The brain matter, flesh, and skull were visible in the hunk of his head that I'd lopped off. As it slid away from his body, the blood rushed out. There was so much, that it obscured all other details.

"I gotta get the fuck out of here," I said.

Wiping down the sword, I threw it into the fireplace, hoping to remove any traces of myself. I was a hard-to-find kind of guy, but my prints were in the system.

I removed the security guard's pants and shoes. The pants were a little big on me, but the shoes actually fit. I lifted the machine gun off the floor, and looked it over, preparing myself to use it.

I closed the door, stuffed the barrel into a pillow on the couch, and began to fiddle with all the gun mechanisms. It took me several minutes to realize an Uzi has two safeties. After firing a pair of shots into the sofa, I listened to see if anyone had heard me. Nothing. I readied myself, figuring I shouldn't wait around any longer than I had to.

I returned to Rodger and sifted through the pants around his ankles, locating his wallet, a money clip, and a key ring. The ring appeared to contain several sets of car keys, one to a Cadillac.

"Just my style," I said. "I need to find the garage."

It had been a while since I'd spoken out loud in front of people. Even though these were dead people, it still made me feel powerful. So did the machine gun.

I scoured the inside of the mansion, peering around each corner until I found a side exit to the house.

In front of the garage sat several cars. I pressed one of the fobs on his keychain to see if I could get a hit.

The lights on the black Cadillac flashed. "Come to Daddy," I whispered.

I ran over to the car and slipped inside. Setting the Uzi down on the passenger seat, I quickly jammed the key in the ignition. When I started it up, gunfire caused the back window to explode. I slumped down in the chair, adjusting the back mirror between bursts.

Off in the distance, I could see a pair of men letting off shots on the grass lawn. I threw the car into reverse and stomped on the gas. As I got closer to the men, they prepared to dodge. But instead of backing straight into them, I cut the wheel. The half-moon swing sent the front end of the Caddy into one guy's legs, causing him to helicopter end-over-end before landing on his neck.

More gunfire rained through my windshield, I reversed and swung the car around again, keeping one hand on the wheel and lifting the Uzi with the other, I rounded my way back in the direction of the gunfire. The man was still on the lawn and reloading. It was the perfect opportunity.

I stuck the gun out the driver's side window, using the side mirror to keep it steady. As I ran over the head of the crippled guard I'd just hit, I squeezed the trigger. Bullets erupted and shells jumped. Crimson mist sprayed out of the guard ahead of me, blowing several holes in his chest and head. He fell on his back, most likely already dead, but I still ran over his torso for good measure.

My eyes found the front gate, and it was wide open. As the guard's bones exploded under the weight of the Caddy, I set the machine gun on the passenger seat, white-knuckled the wheel, and headed for the exit.

SOLICITATION

Harvey Sutton, September 1993

Having money made me feel hollow. I had been wanting to share it with other people. Particularly women. Especially, the ones that wanted to give up a piece of ass in return.

The girl walking her dog was no hooker, but it would only be a matter of time until one eventually strolled by. That street had never failed me before.

But looking at the dog made me immediately think back to my time as one. In a way, that night with Rodger changed everything for me. Sure, it left a fuck-load of trauma, but I had plenty of that to begin with.

Hell, I'd seen the aftermath of my own mother stabbing my father. The holes in his chest were still clear in my mind. The haunting echo of her laughter accompanied them from time to time.

I'd watched several men fuck and abuse a corpse that I dug up from a graveyard. A rotten husk that I hid under a bridge like a dog buries a bone. This woman—a woman I respected, nonetheless—was a hero. A tier of tough I'd aspired to achieve. She'd scraped her way out of all this bullshit. I knew why I'd pimped her body out. It was survival of the fittest. But I still couldn't figure out why *I'd* fucked her.

Maybe it was to make her feel better as I'd told her—and myself. But still, I didn't quite believe it. It had hurt being alone with no one to love and no one to love me. It *still* hurt. There was no denying that's what had brought me back to the streets, longing for some kind of connection with humanity.

Sure, with Bianca, I was fuckin' a corpse. But were these girls *that* much different? Many of them would probably be cashin' out in the near future. Others were already dead on the inside long ago. They were closer to talkin' corpses than actual people.

Piling on a little more fucked up shit on my psyche wasn't really gonna change much. But all the other shit that had changed as a result of these events was mind-blowing.

When I escaped Rodger's home, I had to ditch the car and find some real clothes. The couple grand between his money clip and wallet allowed me to get back on my feet. But it was the thing I'd stolen that I wasn't even aware of that changed my life.

Throughout the entire fight that night, I never realized I was still wearing the human dog collar that Rodger had fashioned for me. The custom piece was made of 14k white gold and littered with diamonds. The diamonds alone were worth close to a hundred thousand dollars.

And suddenly, I was one of them.

It was the weirdest feeling. Despite being able to take care of myself, I wasn't happy. For the first time, I had an apartment, money, and clothes. I didn't have to worry about stealing food or eating out of a dumpster. But there was somethin' missing.

I was alone. But even though I had no one, it still felt like I'd betrayed someone. Maybe I just felt like I'd betrayed myself.

That also might've been why I'd returned to my old stomping grounds. I was only twenty-six, but I felt twice that age. There was something about being in those same shitty streets and going back to the site of my trauma that helped. Interacting with the people trapped like I had been trapped.

Another change in my personality that occurred when I got money was that I stopped thinking about killing all those people. I stopped thinking about what The Dark Man had told me. After my come-up, I finally had a life—something to lose.

I battled with this new ideology though, because despite knowing I needed to protect my future, the rage remained inside me. I had so much anger and hatred from the way the world had treated me. I still very much wanted to see people die.

And after how things went down in prison with Rome and on the outside with Rodger, how was I supposed to feel good about anything? There weren't too many Hallmark moments in my memory to hang my hat on when I got down in the dumps. I'd tend to think about murder and how it might alleviate some of my feelings of unrest instead.

It was while I was thinking about piles of dead people that I saw her. She wore a purple dress that exposed part of her ass and had the same dirty braids and bugged-out eyes. When she stepped up to the edge of the curb, I noticed something else though: her matching high heels. When I saw those purple high heels, my eyes widened. I thought back to the tree. Was it just another coincidence? There must've been millions of purple high heels manufactured every year. I was bound to see a pair, right?

But it wasn't just about the shoes, it was about who was wearing them: Donya Mims was back on the streets.

When I pulled up to her, she got inside the car before either of us said anything.

"Whatchu want?" she asked.

"I want you to tell me how you've been," I replied.

She looked me in the eyes, furrowing her brow and sucking her teeth. "I'm not in the mood for no bullshit tonight."

I'd forgotten about the plastic surgery Rodger had gotten me. I looked like a completely different person. My new look presented me with an interesting choice.

Since I had no one else in my life to recognize me, this was a first. But maybe I could use my new chameleon casing to my advantage—to get an unfiltered, honest look at Donya. Sometimes it's easier to tell a stranger your troubles.

I pulled out a fifty. "I'm serious. I don't want anything from you but to know how you are. Just talk to me a bit."

She snatched the money out of my hand. "I'm hoein'. I'm on the fuckin' street, lost and wandering every day. Sometimes, I wake up disappointed, wishin' I didn't. How's that?"

"I'm sorry," I said. "Why do you think you feel that way? Was it always like that?"

I could tell she was really thinking about the question. "Yes and no. Yes, cuz this ain't my first time out here. No, cuz I…" Her eyes started to gloss over. "I thought I'd actually escaped it. That shows you what a stupid fuckin' bitch I am."

"I don't think you're stupid," I said.

It was hard to see her in such a way. I'd been imagining her in a better place since she'd been on the right track much longer than I had. I didn't want to ask the question, I knew it would hurt her, but I had to.

"What brought you back?"

Donya wiped the tear away from her face. "I had an experience when I was younger. Something that... I-I don't talk about that though. Not even for money."

"Did you ever try keeping a journal?" I asked. "I recently found out that, sometimes, writing about that kind of thing can help. Especially with the older stuff."

"I ain't got paper to wipe my fuckin' ass with, you think I got a pen and a book?"

I realized something in that moment. Just because I had money, it didn't mean it was thanks to anyone else. No one helped me. And just because I was on the upswing, it didn't mean that I couldn't get turned on my head at any given moment.

There was no better example than the woman sitting beside me. Donya was a different fuckin' person when I was back upstate looking at her through that glass. And now, she was no further along than when we were kids.

"Well, things can change," I replied.

"I'm aware," she said.

"I think you and I are a lot alike."

"Yeah, how's that?"

"I'd be willin' to bet that you were feelin' just as empty when things were good. Just as empty as when things aren't so good."

She turned to me, drawn in by my statement.

"And do you know why?" I asked.

"Why?" she asked.

"Because we ain't gonna be right until we listen to what we were told. Otherwise, that night in the warehouse is gonna haunt us both forever."

I could see the shock on Donya's face. Her jaw chattered as she searched for words. "How do you know about that?"

I grinned. "Because your big brother's back."

IDENTITY THEFT

Harvey Sutton, May 1994

When I got back in the car, Donya and I examined the ID card. Sure, it was a fake, but at the same time, it wasn't. It was a genuine ID, just with my picture and information. It was better to go the extra mile, take a bit more time, and ensure we had a legit in.

Since that night, when I'd broken it all down, Donya was even more enthusiastic than me to get our plan moving. I'm not sure if she actually believed I was Harvey Sutton or if she thought this was just The Dark Man's prophecy coming true, but she was inspired like I'd never seen.

Sure, we were both partying a bit since I had some money—smokin' crack, fuckin' raw, drinkin' almost nonstop—but when it came to the business side of things, she was more focused than I ever remember her being. More focused than when I saw her on the other side of that glass.

Donya held up the ID card of a maintenance worker named Martin Weiss for comparison. "Looks perfect."

We had been working on gathering all the intel and supplies and getting things to fall into place for over a half year now. The last item on our bucket list was stealing the crew card. It was our final piece of preparation.

"So, when do you think you should stash the shit?" Donya asked.

It was a good question.

"I think the closer to our vacation the better," I said. "The less time that it's onboard, the less time they have to find it."

"Makes sense."

We sat there in silence for another few moments, like we were both waiting for something but didn't know what.

"You ever think about going back?" I finally asked.

She exhaled. It sounded like there was a lot on her mind. "Yeah, but I'm not sure we'd ever get there."

"We could always buy more LSD," I said. "You know, just to be sure about this. You know what I mean?"

"No, you don't get it."

"Well tell me then."

"I'm sayin' that specific sheet of acid we dropped was different. After we took it, I couldn't stop thinkin' about what we seen. I knew somethin' had to be up."

"So?"

"So, I asked around. Eventually, I figured out where it came from." She shook her head and paused.

"It's like pullin' fuckin' teeth with you sometimes. Just tell me what the deal is, would ya?"

"You wouldn't believe me if I did, but I swear it's the truth."

"Try me."

"J-Roc, the dealer I lifted the tabs off, he ain't buy it off no hippie or create it in some fuckin' basement. He didn't even have to pay for it. It was given to him."

I rolled my eyes. "Okay, I'll bite. By who?"

She swallowed, as if trying to will herself to finally spit it out. "By the United States government."

I laughed. "Get the fuck outta here. Why the fuck would the government wanna pay to make LSD then just hand it out for free?"

She shrugged. "Your guess is as good as mine. But they did."

"Says who?"

"The streets. This ain't just one person who told me this shit. Word is they also created crack and be pushin' that too."

I wanted to brush off her response but living a decent life for the past several years had distorted my view. I realized that I was thinking like one of them, not like one of us. Everybody lies, but the streets don't.

"Then… then what do you think all of that shit was?" I asked.

I thought back to The Dark Man and all the vivid hallucinations from our night of darkness. There seemed to be a certain prophetic nature to my journey, but I couldn't tell if it was just me forcing the puzzle pieces into a certain position or if they naturally fit into place. The bombshell Donya dropped had fucked up my whole way of thinking.

"All what shit?" Donya asked.

"You know," I said, "our shared hallucination that night in the warehouse."

Donya looked me dead in the eyes. I'd never seen her so serious. "It was fate."

"I been sayin' that, but what the fuck does that actually mean?" I was losing my patience with her. My fuse was burning down. "Just give it to me straight. It's been on my mind for years! I don't just wanna know. I *need* to."

She wasn't rattled by my outburst. I could tell there was a look of familiarity in her eyes—like she'd been in my shoes before.

"Chill, big brother," she replied. "Remember, you and I'll fight the world and ourselves, but never each other. You remember that, right?"

"Yeah, I remember. And I would never fight you, but you already know that."

"I know." Donya smiled, slipping the ID cards into her pocket.

"But just tell me what you mean, please. I'm beggin' you."

"Okay, but it ain't good news, you know that, right?"

"Good news ain't never been a part of my life anyhow."

"I'm only sayin' this shit because once you know, you're always gonna know. And sometimes, not knowin' is all that keeps us sane."

"I get it," I growled. "I'm willin' to take the fuckin' risk. As if there was a way to be more miserable than I already am."

"Understood," Donya said. "Well, what I meant was *exactly* what I said. There ain't no stoppin' fate."

I squinted my eyes, believing I finally understood what she was saying. "Are... are you trying to tell me that the U.S. government created a drug with the power to alter our fuckin' futures?"

Donya laughed and shook her head. "That's a nice way to think of it, but that wouldn't be so bad, would it? That would make *them* the bad guys, right?"

I nodded.

Her face tightened and eyes grew deathly serious. "But they ain't the fuckin' bad guys, Harv. We are."

When she said that, I instantly felt light-headed and nauseous. A bunch of different ideas ran through my head, yet I still wasn't sure if I fully understood.

Donya recognized I still needed another nudge to enlighten me.

"The way I understand it, that government acid ain't alter our fate. It just showed us what it was."

MASS MURDER

Harvey Sutton, July 1994

As I laid out on the deck taking in some sun, I felt free. Me and Donya were finally taking that vacation we'd never gotten to take. This time, we didn't need a government-altered street drug to get there. We just needed two tickets and each other.

With a capacity of just over two thousand people, the cruise ship was equipped with all the commodities that people dream of. As the sun started to droop and glow orange, I looked over to Donya.

"It's almost time," I said.

She smiled. "I can't wait."

We retired back to our room, knowing we needed to get our heads on straight. First, we fucked. We both wanted to get at least one more in before things inevitably went south. The sex was somehow passionate and soulless at the same time, like a pair of hungry ghouls tearing each other apart.

After showering, we dried off and laid in the bed. I held her in my arms, and we took a nice long nap together, but not before I set the alarm clock for 3:30 AM.

When we woke, the two of us said nothing to each other. After all, what else was there to say? It was time. We were ready. The propulsion system that was the universe pushed us forward.

We both got dressed and looked under the curtain hanging below the bed. I used the boxcutter I'd extracted from my bag to cut through the stitching that resewed the foot of the boxspring back together.

The last time I was in the room was under the guise of the ship mechanic Martin Weiss. I'd cut into the boxspring, hollowing it out and stashing several hard cases inside. I'd affixed some smaller springs atop those cases to try and make it feel natural.

The ship we were on had done a couple of other cruises since I'd planted our stash, but thankfully, no one had been alerted to it or curious enough to randomly cut into the boxspring. It took a few minutes before I had all the cases opened up on the floor.

Two AK-47s, three handguns, and about a dozen motion-activated explosives sat in front of us. The proximity mines were the most expensive. We had to go through a ton of ex-military guys at the shelter before we found one with any knowledge or connection to explosives. But once we did, it was pretty straightforward.

It's incredible what money can buy.

We'd made sure to get a room on the lowest part of the ship so we could work our way up toward the top deck with the explosives. The plan was to drop them close to the exterior of the ship, one or two in the hallways on each level.

I kept the AK steady while Donya set the explosives. I was expecting people to pop out of their rooms at any moment, but that didn't happen initially. We'd gotten all the way up to the third floor by the time the first bomb went off.

Panic ensued.

Donya and I both raised our guns up as several doors around us opened.

The one right in front of me contained two women who looked to be related. Their appearances would be even more closely tied together as I held down the trigger and watched the bullets rip through them.

I felt the same euphoric rush I had when I'd done in Rodger. Same as when I was escaping his property and firing off rounds indiscriminately. If that rich prick and his little fuck boys could only see me now.

I heard Donya's gun erupt and a chorus of screams get cut short. As she mowed down several horrified vacationers, suddenly, another explosion went off below us. The ship rumbled, causing us to brace against the walls to maintain our balance.

That second bomb must've motivated the apprehensive people still hunkering down inside their cabins after hearing gunfire. A new wave of people rushed out into the hallway, tripping over each other, fright fuckin' with their ability to function and protect themselves.

It was almost *too* easy.

"This is somethin' ain't it, Harv?" Donya asked.

When I turned to look at her, she was using the backside of her rifle to break open a wounded man's head.

"It's everything we knew it'd be," I said, returning my gaze back down the hallway in front of me.

I noticed a little boy holding his teddy bear in one hand and his father's hand in the other was now the closest warm body to me. The boy was crying hysterically, screaming at the top of his lungs. His father tried to drag him along into the crowd of bloody bodies, but the bullets were too quick.

Several slugs hit the man in the back of his head, sending him toppling forward. The bottleneck of panicked people swallowed up the boy, but I aimed into the area where he should've been. The hot bullets chewed up flesh like hungry homeless people facing a Thanksgiving dinner—the same way me and Donya ate that can of Spam all those years ago during our little Thanksgiving.

Several people hit the floor. Blood and brain matter painted the tight hallway as another explosion went off.

The boat rocked and shifted its angle. I used my arm to bridge myself up and steady my gun.

The little boy sat in a heap of bodies, shrieking something fierce. Blood now covered his entire face. A bullet had blown off part of his cheek. As the injured around him fended for themselves, I was reminded of the selfishness of nearly everyone I'd come across in my time on the planet.

The sight was beyond appropriate.

I looked back at Donya who was reloading. A pile comprised of several families lay on the floor in front of her. There was so much blood in the hallway that the carpets squished when I took my next steps.

I squatted down in front of the boy as he clenched his crimson teddy bear and pulled out my knife.

"Don't cry, little man," I said. "This is just life. Fate in the fuckin' making."

SUICIDE

Harvey Sutton, July 1994

Every captain goes down with his ship.

I captured these final thoughts inside the captain's quarters. I'm not sure anyone will ever learn of or give a fuck about my story, but it'll be here if they want it. Most likely twenty thousand feet below sea level when it's all said and done. But it might be best for Donya and me to be forgotten.

When I look outside the window right now, all I can see is water and darkness. But looking back, all I ever saw was darkness anyhow. Today was just another day. It was a little more beautiful than most, but just another fuckin' day.

Donya and I killed as many men, women, and children as we could. The ones we didn't shoot, either got blown up or jumped overboard. I can't imagine the odds of them surviving to be very good.

I sat down beside Donya on the bed, each with a drink in our hands. We planned to fuck one more time then to go to sleep.

At this time, I'm not exactly sure what to believe. After Donya told me the backstory on the acid, I do wonder how different things might've turned out if we never took it. If the shit she heard on the streets was real, then I guess it wouldn't have mattered anyhow.

I didn't feel much different after the massacre. I didn't feel better or worse. The fact that I didn't feel seemed to lend more credibility to that story. I felt more like some carefully put together wind-up doll than what most people pictured when they thought of a human being.

Yet still, this looming sense of uncertainty persisted. It wasn't anything new of course. I'd been confused and in a constant state of doubt my entire life. But there was a part of me that imagined that would evaporate once I reached the finish line.

One question still haunted me: was it me who led a life of crime, or a life of crime that led me? I don't know. Funny thing though, the color of the captain's bedsheet is gold.

I'M AN '80s BABY

Aron Beauregard, May 2024

I'm an '80s baby and a '90s kid. Most people who have read my work are probably aware of this since the majority of my stories take place in those eras.

For me, that time was just magic. It was a time before cell phones and when the internet was all mysterious and just kicking off. When politics and extreme ideologies weren't so interwoven into the fabric of society. Back then, at least to me, it didn't feel so divided. But I'm sure everyone looks back fondly on the time period when they were young, and it's possible I'm just blinded by nostalgia.

Anyhow, that's not really the point of this essay. The preceding story, *A Life of Crime*, is a tale of choices. It centers around a character named Harvey Sutton, but really, many parts of this story could've been a lot of people.

It could've been me.

When I was younger, I was a knucklehead. I don't believe I was a terrible person, but I hung out around a lot of shady people and made plenty of poor choices.

In my early twenties, I figured I'd just sell drugs to make extra money. My existence was a constant party. Drugs, drinking, sex, and most any reckless behavior was constantly on the agenda. I didn't think about or do anything else. I didn't have any sort of goals or idea where I was headed.

Selling drugs was what everyone around me was doing. It fed into that constant party mentality. It was in the movies we watched, the music we listened to, and the real-life criminals we idolized. It didn't matter that the risk didn't stack up to the reward, it was part of the lifestyle.

It was fuckin' dumb.

But you couldn't have told me that back then. It wouldn't have mattered.

My mind was made up. Maybe that was just part of being a young man and not having a fully developed brain.

Probably a month or so after high school I was working in a pallet factory. Making the wooden pallets that freight gets shipped on. The fuckin' job sucked. I was either sweating or freezing my ass off in the outdoor warehouse. Of course I was going to try and take a shortcut.

I remember getting into the backseat of a car with an Arabic man and picking up a pound of weed. My mother stumbled upon it in my room shortly after—probably due to the smell—and, needless to say, she wasn't happy. She demanded I return it.

Well, a pound of weed doesn't typically come with a receipt. I told her I would but instead took the brick to a friend's house, where I broke it down and bagged it up. I'm choosing to omit this friend's name out of respect as I'm not sure if he'd want this put out there. More on that in just a moment.

To give you an idea of the type of shit going on at the time, this friend had recently just had his house shot up. Probably the scariest part was no one knew exactly why.

Sure, there were theories, but they were just that. When someone's trying to kill you and you don't know the exact angle, that's a bit concerning.

They had attempted to murder him while he was walking home from the bodega. Several shots intended for him went into his neighbor's house as he bolted up the block trying to get cover. A bullet nicked his arm and left a hole in his shirt—it would go on to become his lucky tee.

This friend I'd met in a rap studio. I had dropped a 16 on a track with him, and we just kind of hit it off. I remember the first time I went to his house; the police crime scene tape was still on the porch and driveway from the shooting. This shows you about how smart I was at this time. What kind of idiot shows up to a crime scene and thinks it's a good foundation to build a friendship?

A short time later, I was able to move out on my own, and shit got even crazier. Maybe someday I'll write a book about it. Hopefully I can remember enough still. The myriad of misfortune included people getting pistol whipped, robbed at gunpoint, a home invasion on my 3rd floor apartment, and more.

Anyway, I'm adding that to serve as context to my main point: shit can go south for *anyone*. There were a couple of very specific moments in my life that I look back on as pivotal. If I made one different decision, maybe I'm not alive. Or maybe I'm in prison on some dumb drug shit. Maybe all the books I got the privilege of writing would never have made it to a public audience.

Eventually, I smartened up, but it took a long time. A felony arrest for shrooms, among other things. In a lot of ways, I was leading a life of crime. Until I got enough life experience to understand that I'd allowed myself to be brainwashed.

I never actually looked at it as me being brainwashed until I was talking through it all with my wife while we were hanging out on the couch one night. The glorification and hard push of the lifestyle I'd chosen, to quote Ice Cube, was 'suspicious.'

The wave of Gangsta Rap that dominated the airwaves in the 90s and 2000s was a mass influence on culture everywhere. Rappers like Ice Cube and Krayzie Bone have spoken about how a lot of the exact same people who owned those record labels also own private prisons. Is it definitive proof of brainwashing?

No.

But it is certainly circumstantial.

There are also rappers who claim to have been approached and brought into meetings with these penitentiary people and offered incentives to push a criminal agenda within their music. I'm sure some of this music was organic and just happened, but some was probably manufactured as well.

I'm in no way saying that all my mistakes were purely a result of the music I was listening to or the criminal element and the culture around me. I was a dumb-fuck doing dumb shit. But I do believe it had an impact. That I allowed my psyche to be seduced and very nearly fucked up my entire life as a result.

But thankfully I didn't.

I'm also grateful for my life experience, the people I met, and the wild times we had. I think much of the crazy shit I've seen and had to deal with has made me a much better writer and humbler person.

Going back to my friend from earlier. I said it wasn't a very bright idea to befriend someone in a house covered in crime scene tape, but regardless of whether I should or shouldn't have, I'm glad I did.

He's a great guy who, like myself, had been through a lot of shit. He and I have both moved on from that life of crime.

Now a proud father and family man, I'm sure he reflects on those insane times, fearful for his child. Looking back, he knows today that if his circumstances could've been different, the path he took wouldn't have been so tumultuous. Hopefully, he'll be able to keep the pavement smooth for his kid.

In an abstract way, this is kind of what *A Life of Crime* is about. In life, we all have choices. Our choices are influenced by the things we allow to influence us. A young mind is especially impressionable, and unfortunately, there are a lot more bad influences out there than good ones.

ISSUE 6
THE OBITUARIES
RED ROMANCE
SPECIAL GUEST AUTHOR
C.V. HUNT
DANIEL J. VOLPE · ARON BEAUREGARD · KRISTOPHER TRIANA

COMING FALL 2024!

STAB
THE
RABBIT
Shane McKenzie

MCHORROR.NET

If you are interested in the butthead who penned my introduction, Shane McKenzie, I recommend checking out his website. Shaners' first release, *Stab the Rabbit,* will include an exclusive preview of our upcoming extreme horror novel *Benjamin.* If you enjoyed the gritty pulp tale you just read, then Benjamin is gonna absolutely blow your balls off! If you don't have balls, then it will fry your fuckin' eggs. The shit is guaranteed! If your balls aren't blown or eggs ain't fried, Shane promises to do the job himself! How fuckin' cool is that?!

NEW HARDCOVER!

ABOUT THE AUTHOR

Aron Beauregard is a guy who easily could've taken a wrong turn in life. He's grateful for all his readers and the writing career that he is fortunate enough to have. There is not a day that he wakes up and doesn't appreciate his readers and the people who believe(d) in him. They alone are the force propelling him forward.